HOW MANY SPOTS DOES A LEOPARD HAVE?

and Other Tales

by Julius Lester

illustrated by David Shannon

SCHOLASTIC INC.

NEW YORK   TORONTO   LONDON   AUCKLAND   SYDNEY

To Deena
— J.L. —

To my wife,
Heidi
— D.S. —

ISBN 0-590-41972-2

12 11 10 9 8 7 6 5 4 3 2 1   2   4 5 6 7 8 9/9
Printed in the U.S.A.   09

Contents

HOW MANY SPOTS DOES A LEOPARD HAVE?
And Other Tales

Why The Sun And The Moon Live In The Sky

IN THE TIME OF THE BEGINNING OF BEGINNINGS, everything and everyone lived on earth. If you had been living in those times, you could've sat on your porch in the evening and watched the Sun, the Moon and the Stars taking a stroll and chatting with all the neighbors.

The Sun had many friends, but his best friend in all the universe was Water. Every day Sun visited Water and they talked about this and that and enjoyed each other's company, which is what friends do.

There was one thing wrong with their friendship, however. Water never came to visit Sun at his house. That hurt Sun's feelings.

He could've held onto his hurt feelings and gotten angry. But that's not the way to treat your feelings when they're hurt. You feel better if you talk to the one who hurt them. Maybe Water didn't know that he had hurt Sun's feelings.

"Why don't you ever visit me?" Sun asked Water.

"I would love to visit you," Water replied, "but your house might not be big enough for me and all of my relatives. I wouldn't want to force you out of your house. If you want me to visit, you must build a very, very, very, very, very large house. I need a lot of room."

Sun went home and told his wife, the Moon, that they had to build a very, very, very, very, very large house. His friend, Water, was coming to visit.

They set to work immediately. He sawed. She nailed. He hammered. She measured, and they built a very, very, very, very, very large house indeed.

The house was so large that it took a whole day to walk from the front door to the back door. The house was so wide that when you stood on one side, you couldn't see the other side.

Sun went and told Water that he could come visit now.

The next morning Water flowed up the road. "Is it safe to come in?" he asked when he got to the house.

"Please enter," said Sun and Moon, opening the door to the house they had built.

Water began flowing in. With him came the fish and all the other water creatures.

Soon the water was knee-deep. "Is it still safe for me to come in?"

"Of course," Sun and Moon said.

More water flowed in. Soon it was halfway to the ceiling. "Do you want more of me to come in?"

"Of course," said Sun and Moon, rising to the ceiling so they wouldn't get wet and have their lights put out.

More water and more water and more water flowed in. Sun and Moon had to go sit on the roof.

"Do you want more of me to come in?" asked Water.

Sun and Moon said yes, not knowing what they were saying.

More and more Water poured in. With him came more and more fish and whales and sharks and seaweed and crabs and lobsters. Water covered the roof of the house and got higher and higher.

How Many Spots Does A Leopard Have?

The higher Water rose, the higher in the sky Sun and Moon had to go to stay dry.

Finally Sun and Moon were so high in the sky they weren't sure how to get down. But they liked being so high up and looking down on the world.

And that's where they've been ever since.

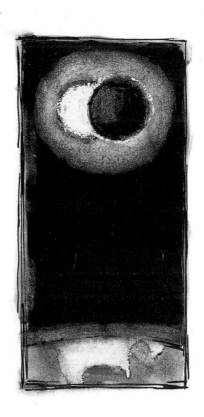

The Bird That Made Milk

 NCE A GREAT FAMINE CAME UPON THE LAND. DAY after day the sun burned hot. The people had nothing to eat except the grain they had saved from the previous year's harvest and there was not much of that. They ate enough each day to keep from starving, but they were always hungry. Before long everyone became as thin as ribbons.

In the land was a man named Masilo. Each day he worked in the field next to his house with his wife, Adisa. They knew nothing would grow. However, if rain should fall, their field would be prepared.

One evening after they stopped working, a bird flew through the sky and lighted on top of their house. The bird sang out, "All the earth that they have tilled, come together."

The ground did as the bird said, and all the work Masilo and Adisa had done was as if it had never been.

The next morning when Masilo and Adisa came to the field, they could not find the place where they had tilled the day before.

"There is something wrong here," Masilo said, but he did not know what it was.

He and his wife worked all that day. When they went into

their house that evening the bird flew through the sky, landed on top of the house and sang, "All the earth that they have tilled, come together."

And it was so.

The next morning when Masilo and Adisa came to the field, the earth looked as if it had never been touched. Masilo and Adisa began to wonder if a witch had put a spell on them and their land.

That evening when they finished, Masilo said to Adisa, "You go into the house. I will stay and watch. I want to find out who or what is undoing our hard work."

Masilo hid in the bushes at the head of the field and waited.

Before long he saw a bird fly through the sky and land on top of the house. It was a beautiful bird with black and golden feathers. Masilo was admiring the bird, when suddenly the bird spoke. "All the earth that they have tilled, come together."

And it was so.

Masilo was angry. Quickly and quietly, he climbed the ladder that leaned against the house and with the speed of a striking snake, he caught the bird.

"So it is you who makes us do the same work over and over each day."

Masilo took out his knife and was about to cut off the bird's head.

"Wait! Wait!" pleaded the bird. "Please don't kill me. If you let me live, I will make milk for you and your family to drink."

"Not before you undo what you have just done."

"Let the tilled earth reappear," the bird said.

And it was so.

"That's better. Now, let's see this milk you were talking about."

Suddenly milk began flowing into Masilo's hands. He drank. It was rich and cool and so delicious.

Masilo took the bird into the house. "Wash all of our pots," he told his wife.

His wife wondered why Masilo wanted the pots. You didn't need more than one pot to cook the little bird Masilo had in his hand. But she washed the pots.

Masilo took the bird and said, "Make milk."

The bird filled all the pots with milk.

Masilo, Adisa, and their children drank. When they finished, they were no longer hungry.

Adisa and the children had many questions about how Masilo had found such a miraculous bird, but all he said was, "Do not tell anyone about this bird."

Adisa and the children swore they would tell no one.

Each day Masilo and his family drank the milk the bird made. Before long, they looked fat and healthy.

The people of the village wondered why Masilo and his family looked healthy while everyone else looked poor. "Masilo must know where there is food," they said.

The people watched Masilo and his family carefully to see where they were getting food, but they did not discover the secret.

One day the children of the village were playing outside Masilo's house. "Why are you fat when we are thin?" someone asked Masilo's children.

"Are we fat?" Masilo's children wondered. "We thought we were thin like you."

"No, you look fat and rich. We look thin and poor. Where are you getting your food?"

Masilo's children replied, "We cannot tell you."

The other children kept asking and kept asking. Finally

Masilo's children said, "There is a miraculous bird in our house who makes milk."

"Can we see?" the other children asked.

All the children went inside the house. Masilo's children brought the bird out from its secret place.

"Make milk," they ordered the bird and it did. Everyone drank the milk and for the first time in weeks, their stomachs did not hurt with hunger.

The children were so happy that they began to play with the bird, chasing it from one side of the room to the other. The bird began bumping into the walls. Afraid that the bird might hurt itself, the children opened the door so they could play with the bird outside.

When the bird saw the open door, it did not hesitate. Before the children realized it, the bird was a speck in the distant and high sky.

Masilo's children were very afraid. "Our father will be very angry with us for letting the bird escape. We must go after it and bring it back."

The children of the village said, "It is our fault that your miraculous bird escaped. We will go with you."

That evening when the parents came home, their children were gone. No one knew where they were, or what had happened to them.

When Masilo and Adisa came home, their children were gone, and so was the bird. Masilo knew what had happened, and he and Adisa were very sad.

The children were sad, too. Night was coming and they were far from the village. Suddenly a big storm came and the skies flashed with lightning and the thunder crashed and the children were very afraid, except for the oldest of the boys, who said, "Do not be afraid. I know how to make a house appear."

"Hurry and do it," the other children said.

"House appear!"

And it was so.

The children went inside the house and built a great fire and they were safe from the storm.

After the storm passed, they heard a loud voice from outside.

"I am the Monster Who Eats Children and I smell children inside this house. Open the door and let me in!"

The monster banged on the door so hard that the house began shaking.

"What are we going to do?" the children wanted to know.

The oldest boy went to the back of the house. "Make door," he said.

A door appeared. He opened it and the children ran out as fast as they could. They ran and they ran and the Monster Who Eats Children ran close behind them.

Soon the children were tired. They climbed to the top of a tall tree. The monster began cutting down the tree with his long fingernails.

The oldest boy told the children to sing with him: "Tree be strong! Tree be strong!"

Over and over the children sang. Each time they did, the tree became solid again where the monster was cutting it.

After a while the children were tired and out of breath from singing, and The Monster Who Eats Children cut more and more of the tree away. The tree began to weaken and sway.

Then, out of the sky, came a flock of birds, each one with beautiful black and golden feathers.

The Bird That Made Milk

The birds landed in the top of the tree. "Get on our backs," they said to the children.

Even though the birds were small, they were very strong. The children got on their backs and the birds carried them back to their village. The parents were very happy to see their children and the children were happy to see their parents. The parents were even happier when the children told them that these were miraculous birds who could make milk.

Each house in the village had its own bird and everyone had milk to drink. Soon everyone looked fat and healthy.

When the famine ended, all the birds flew away.

No one ever saw them again.

The Monster
Who Swallowed
Everything

NCE UPON A TIME THERE LIVED A MONSTER NAMED
Ko-Domo-Domo. He was as big as a mountain
and hair grew out of his body like grass. He had
one green eye and one yellow eye and the eye in
the middle of his forehead was red. Every time one of his big
smelly feet landed on the ground, the earth shook. Ko-Domo-
Domo was feared by everyone because he swallowed everything in his path.

The people did not know what to do. Ko-Domo-Domo had
swallowed the entire country except for three small villages
in a valley beneath the mountain pass.

The day came when the people in the valley were awakened
by the earth trembling. Ko-Domo-Domo was coming!

The people in the first village tried to run to the second
village but it was no use. With arms as long as a streak of
lightning, Ko-Domo-Domo reached down and picked up all
the people, the cows, the goats, the sheep, the dogs, the
chickens and all the houses and barns and swallowed them,
each and every one.

He gave a loud belch and went to the second village and
swallowed it.

How Many Spots Does A Leopard Have?

Only one village was left. In that village a woman was about to have a baby. Feeling the earth quiver and shiver at the approach of Ko-Domo-Domo, the woman hurried into a cave. She listened as Ko-Domo-Domo swept the village into his hands and swallowed it. She was afraid that the monster would find her inside the cave, but her fear was replaced by the baby whose time to be born had come.

The woman gave birth to a baby boy. Laying him on the ground, she began looking around the cave for something to make a bed with for him.

A few minutes later she returned with an armful of pine needles. But her baby was not there. Where her baby had been lying was a fully grown man.

"Where is my child?" the woman asked anxiously.

"I am your child," the man answered in a deep voice.

"But, I don't understand. A moment ago you were an infant. Now you are grown. How?"

The man shook his head. "I do not know. The ways of the gods are not to be understood by such as we. I feel the earth trembling as if the world were about to die. What is going on?"

"The great monster, Ko-Domo-Domo, has destroyed our land."

The man, whose name was Dit-a-Lane, went outside. The land was desolate. Not a house or barn remained standing.

He looked toward the horizon where the path between the mountains led into and out of the valley. There he saw a strange sight — a mountain bigger than the mountains surrounding the valley. He looked closely. He couldn't believe what he saw.

What he had thought was a mountain was not. It was the

monster, Ko-Domo-Domo, who had grown even larger after swallowing the three villages. Ko-Domo-Domo had gotten so large that he was stuck in the mountain pass that led to and from the valley.

Dit-a-Lane found some spears and he marched toward Ko-Domo-Domo. The monster opened his huge mouth and growled. Dit-a-Lane threw the spears into Ko-Domo-Domo's mouth. The monster screamed and then died.

But the monster was still stuck in the entrance to the valley. Dit-a-Lane took a knife and began cutting the monster in order to remove him.

"Hey!" Dit-a-Lane heard a voice.

He stopped cutting.

"That's better. You could hurt somebody with that knife," came the muffled voice.

Dit-a-Lane started to cut another place on the monster's body. He heard a cow moo. Then he heard dogs barking and goats bleating and chickens cackling. They were all inside Ko-Domo-Domo.

Dit-a-Lane cut very carefully. Soon he had cut the monster open. Out came all the people and all the animals that Ko-Domo-Domo had swallowed. They were happy to be freed. They searched around inside the monster until they found their houses and belongings.

Then everybody went off and rebuilt their villages. The country that had been dead came back to life. The people were so happy that they made Dit-a-Lane their leader and they brought him many gifts. He became a wealthy man and ruled wisely for many years.

Tug-Of-War

HAVE YOU EVER NOTICED HOW THE LITTLEST THINGS have the most mouth? Seems like the smaller they are the more mouth they have.

Like Turtle. Anybody who listened to Turtle without seeing him would've thought he was the biggest and baddest thing to ever set foot on the earth.

"I am as powerful as Elephant on dry land. I am as powerful as Hippopotamus in the water. And I've got more brains in my little head than they have in both of their big heads."

Bluejay had been listening to Turtle talking to himself and he flew as fast as he could fly to tell Elephant what Turtle had said.

Elephant was not impressed. "I'm not going to let something as little as Turtle upset me. Let him talk all he wants. I don't care."

Bluejay hurried to the river to tell Hippopotamus. Hippopotamus said the same thing.

Bluejay flew back and told Turtle that Elephant and Hippopotamus said that he was nothing but mouth.

"What?!" shouted Turtle. "How dare they make fun of me? I'll show them! I will! I will! I am their equal. When I get through with them, they will call me Friend."

How Many Spots Does A Leopard Have?

Turtle went to look for Elephant and Hippopotamus.

Elephant was lying down in the forest and he looked like a mountain. His trunk was ten years long, his ears were as big as a thunderstorm and his feet were bigger than a broken heart.

None of that impressed Turtle.

"Hey! Get up, big dummy! Your friend is here. Is this any way to greet a friend who has come from a long way to greet you?"

Elephant opened one eye, saw Turtle and stood up. He was so big that, for a minute, the sun was afraid it would have to move higher in the sky.

"Small person! Who are you calling friend?"

"You, big head and little brain! Aren't you my friend?"

"No!" bellowed Elephant. "Who do you think you are, going around saying that you are my equal? Let me step on you and we'll see how equal you are."

Turtle laughed. "What does that have to do with being equal? You think because you're bigger, you're smarter and stronger. Tell you what! Let's have a tug-of-war and find out."

"Why?" Elephant wanted to know. "There's no way you can beat me, half pint."

"So, if you can't lose, what's the big deal? If you pull me over, you're the greatest. If I pull you over, I'm the greatest. But if neither one of us wins, we're friends. Deal?"

Elephant shrugged. "You can call me greatest now and save both of us a lot of time."

Turtle ignored Elephant and went into the forest and cut a long vine. "This is your end," he said to Elephant. "I'm going to go off with my end. We'll start tugging. We won't stop to eat or sleep and we'll pull until one of us wins or the vine breaks."

Turtle went off with the other end of the vine and found Hippopotamus bathing in the river.

"Hey! You! You're supposed to be my friend, but you haven't even come out of the water to say, 'Nice day.'"

Hippopotamus bellowed and splashed angrily in the water. "Your brain must be as hard as your shell if you think you're my friend."

"Not only am I your friend, tadpole brain, I am your equal in strength and in sense. And I'll prove it to you," declared Turtle.

"How?"

"Simple. We'll have a tug-of-war. If you pull me over, you're the greatest. If I pull you over, I'm the greatest. If neither one of us can pull the other one over, then we're equals and can call each other friend. Once the contest starts, we will not eat or sleep until the outcome is decided."

Hippopotamus thought this was one of the stupidest ideas he'd ever heard, but he wanted to show Turtle who was the boss, so he agreed.

Turtle gave Hippopotamus the other end of the rope. Then he went to the middle of the vine, which was where neither Elephant nor Hippopotamus could see him. He shook the vine. When he did that, Elephant pulled at his end and Hippopotamus pulled at his end and the tug-of-war was on.

For a while the vine was taut. Then it began to move a little to Elephant's side. Then it began to pull back toward Hippopotamus's side. Then it moved back toward the middle, not moving in either direction.

Turtle went home and had a big lunch. Then he took a

long nap. Late that afternoon he woke up. "I wonder if those two fools are still pulling on that vine."

He went back to the middle of the vine. The rope was still taut, which meant that neither Elephant nor Hippopotamus was winning.

Turtle was bored. He took his knife and cut the vine.

KER-BLAM-BLAM-A-BLAM! That was what it sounded like when the vine gave way and Elephant fell backward into the woods.

KER-SPLASH-SPLASHY-SPLASHY! That's what it sounded like when the vine gave way and Hippopotamus fell backward into the water.

Turtle went to see Elephant who was looking sad and rubbing his leg.

"Turtle, I didn't know you were that strong," he said. "When the vine broke, I fell and hurt my leg. Well, there is no doubt that we are equals. I apologize for treating you so badly. We are friends, indeed."

Turtle smiled and went down to the river to see what Hippopotamus had to say.

When he got there Hippopotamus was rubbing his head. "Turtle, I did not know you were that strong. When the vine broke I fell and I bumped my head. I apologize, Turtle, for my previous conduct. We are friends, indeed."

Ever afterwards, whenever the animals held a meeting, Elephant, Hippopotamus, and Turtle sat together in the tallest chairs. Whenever they spoke to one another, they called each other Friend.

What do *you* think? Do you think Elephant, Hippopotamus, and Turtle were equals?

Why Dogs Chase Cats

ONG BEFORE THIS TIME WE CALL TODAY, AND before that time called yesterday, and even before "What time is it?" the world wasn't like it is now.

Long before time wound its watch and started ticking and chasing after tomorrow, which it can never catch up to, well, that was the time when Dog and Cat were friends. There weren't two creatures in creation who were better friends than Dog and Cat. From sunup to sundown, from moonup to moondown, Dog and Cat did everything together and never a cross word passed between them.

That's how matters stood until hard times came to visit and decided to stay awhile. Hard times are what you have when you look in your dinner plate and all you see is your face looking back at you.

After a few days of not finding anything to eat, Dog and Cat knew they had to do something. But what?

They scratched their fleas and thought. They thought and scratched each other's fleas. They stopped thinking and stopped scratching. That was when Dog got an idea.

"There's only one thing we can do."

"What's that?" Cat wanted to know.

"We must go our separate ways. It's easier for one to find food than it is for two."

Cat agreed.

"I know where you can find food," Dog continued.

"Where?" Cat asked eagerly.

"Go to Adam's house."

"What will you do?"

"Don't worry about me," Dog said. "I'll find something somewhere."

"But what if you don't?" Cat wondered.

"Well, maybe I'll have to come to Adam's house."

That was what Cat was afraid of. "You eat more than I do. If you come where I am, you'll eat everything and there won't be enough for me. We have to promise that we will never look for food in the place where the other one is."

Dog promised and Cat promised and the two friends went their separate ways.

Cat went to Adam's house. When Eve saw Cat sitting on the back porch she thought he was the cutest thing she'd ever seen. She picked him up, put him on her lap and started stroking him. When night came, Eve brought Cat to bed with her. Adam didn't like the idea of sleeping in the same bed with an animal, but he didn't want to get into an argument with Eve about it.

In the middle of the night, Adam was awakened suddenly by a noise. He sat up. By the light of the moon, he saw Cat catching a mouse. Seeing how useful Cat was going to be, Adam treated him very kindly from that day on, and Cat was never hungry because there were many mice to catch.

Dog was not as lucky. The first night after he and Cat

separated, Dog went to the cave of Wolf and asked for shelter.

Wolf said he was welcome to stay but not to ask for any food. Wolf scarcely had enough for himself.

Dog found a spot near the front of the cave, settled down and went to sleep. Everybody knows that Dog has the best hearing of almost any animal in the world. Dog could hear a raindrop fall on cotton.

In the darkest part of the night, the time of night that's so scary even Moon wishes she had someplace to hide, Dog woke up suddenly.

He listened. He heard trees and bushes being torn out of the ground and footsteps in the distance. He ran to the back of the cave where Wolf was sleeping.

"Something is coming!"

"If you run it away, I'll give you some of my food."

Dog ran back to the front of the cave and waited. The footsteps got louder and louder until out of the forest, holding a tree in each hand, came Gorilla.

Dog growled his growliest growl. He rushed at Gorilla and barked his barkiest bark. Gorilla looked down, picked Dog up and threw him over his shoulder. It was three days and five nights before Dog came down to earth.

Poor Dog didn't know what to do. He wandered and he wandered but no one had more than a few scraps of food to share with him. He was so hungry there was nothing to do but go to Adam's house.

When Adam saw Dog in the backyard, he immediately liked him. He gave Dog something to eat. After he'd filled his stomach, Dog crawled underneath the porch and went to sleep.

In the middle of the night, Dog woke up suddenly. He heard

something! He started barking. Adam awoke, grabbed his bow and arrow and hurried outside. There, in the darkness, he saw a rhinocehorse. Adam shot arrows at it and drove the rhinocehorse away.

Adam patted Dog on the head and told him he could stay forever. His barking had saved Adam's and Eve's lives.

The next morning when Eve put Cat outside, the first thing Cat saw was Dog lying beneath a shade tree.

"What're you doing here?" Cat asked angrily.

Dog started explaining about what a hard time he'd had and how there was more than enough food at Adam's for the two of them.

Cat didn't want to hear a word. "We made a promise and you broke it."

"Let's go to Adam and maybe he can solve our problem," Dog suggested.

Adam listened while Cat said his say. Then he listened to Dog say his say. When each had finished saying their say, it was Adam's turn to say.

"Dog, let there be no mistake. You and Cat made a promise and you broke it. However, Cat, you must understand that I am the one who told Dog he could stay here. There is more than enough food for both of you. I need both of you. Cat, you are useful for catching mice. Dog, you warn me when danger is around. I want you both to stay."

"No!" said Cat. "No, no, no!"

"Why?" Adam asked.

"Because," said Cat, "a promise is a promise."

Dog pleaded with Cat. He reminded Cat that they had been best friends since water was wet. Nothing Dog said could change Cat's mind.

Finally Adam said to Dog, "I'm sorry, but you're going to have to go."

"Where can I go?" Dog wanted to know.

"My son, Seth, lives down the road and around the curve."

So Dog went to live with Seth and he was very happy there.

But from that time to this, whenever a dog sees a cat, he chases after it because he still wants the cat to be his friend.

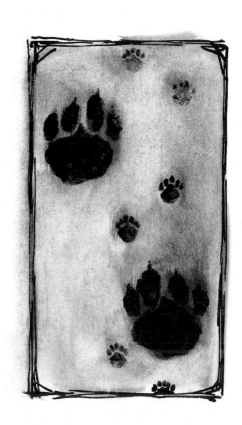

The Town Where Snoring Was Not Allowed

ONE EVENING, JUST AS THE SUN WAS PULLING DOWN the shade and getting ready for bed, two brothers came to a village. They asked who the chief was and where he lived. It was the custom that whenever strangers came to a village, they had to greet the chief first and ask his permission to stay.

The two brothers were shown the way to the chief's house, where they asked if they could stay the night.

"You may spend the night in our village guest house. As soon as you are settled, I will have food brought to you."

The two brothers were very pleased. They had been traveling all day and were very tired. All they wanted to do was eat and go to sleep.

"However, there is something important you must know," the chief continued. "Snoring is not permitted in our village. Anyone who snores will be killed as he sleeps."

The two brothers looked at each other. How could a person control his snoring? It was impossible. The brothers wanted to leave and go to the next village, but night had already risen and was walking through the land. They had to accept the chief's hospitality.

They ate and settled down for the night. Being very tired, they were asleep at once.

They had not been sleeping long when one of them was awakened by a noise. He sat up and listened.

ZZZZZZ! ZZZZZZ!

His brother was snoring!

ZZZZZZ! ZZZZZZ!

Then he heard another sound, a soft, steely sound.

SSSSSSS! SSSSSSS!

The villagers were sharpening their knives! In a few moments they would come to kill the snorer.

The brother who was awake had to do something, but what? He started singing as loudly as he could:

> *Zzzzzz, Zzzzzz, Zzzzzz!*
> *We traveled many miles.*
> *We came to this village.*
> *We were welcomed here.*
> *Zzzzzz, Zzzzzz, Zzzzzz!*

He sang in a loud and strong voice, so loud that the people could not hear the snoring. They put down their knives and began dancing to the music. Someone brought out the drums and began playing rhythms behind the singing. Soon the people were singing the song as well as dancing.

All night one brother snored, one brother sang and the people of the village sang and danced and had a party.

The next morning after the sun had chased the night away, the two brothers went to the chief to tell him good-bye.

The chief was very happy to see them. He was so happy that he gave them a large sack of gold. "This is yours. Never

have I nor my people enjoyed ourselves as much as we did last night dancing to your song. We may be a little sleepy today but we are also very happy because of the fine entertainment you brought to us. Please accept this gold as a sign of our gratitude."

The two brothers left with the gold, very pleased.

Once they were away from the village, however, they began to argue.

"I should get the larger share of this gold," said the brother who had stayed up all night singing. "If it hadn't been for my song, the villagers would not have danced and we would not have been given the gold."

The other brother disagreed. "I think we should share the gold, but I should have the larger share. If I had not snored, you would not have made up the song and we would not have been given the gold."

The brother who had sang thought for a moment. "That is true. If you had not snored, I would not have made up the song. But if I had not made up the song, you would now be dead. I saved your life. For that alone, I deserve the larger share."

The two argued back and forth, back and forth, and could not decide.

Who do you think should have the largest share of gold?

The Town
Where Sleeping Was
Not Allowed

ELL, I CAN'T DECIDE WHO SHOULD GET THE MOST gold, and neither could the two brothers. They argued and argued for many miles without finding a solution.

By the time the sun was getting ready for bed, the two brothers were very tired, especially the one who had stayed up all night singing. He could hardly keep his eyes open.

They came to a village, and went to the chief and asked permission to stay the night.

The chief greeted them warmly and said they were welcome to stay the night. "However, there is one thing you should know. In this village sleeping is not permitted. Anyone who falls asleep is buried immediately."

The sleepy brother could not believe his ears. What awful luck they were having! One night they were in a village where they would kill you for snoring. The next night they were in a village where you would be killed for sleeping.

What was he going to do? He was so sleepy that his head kept dropping forward. What was he going to do?

The two brothers were taken to the guest house and the chief had a large meal sent to them.

"We must not eat all this food," said the brother who had

slept the night before. "If we do, we will become very drowsy and will not be able to stay awake."

"But I am hungry," said the other brother. "I am so hungry and so tired. All day long I have been looking forward to a large meal and long sleep."

And he ate all the food. When he finished, he yawned and stretched. "I feel much better now. I think I will take a little nap. No one will mind if I have just a little nap."

"No! You mustn't. They will kill you if you fall asleep. You must do push-ups and exercises so you can stay awake."

The sleepy brother stretched himself out on the floor and started doing push-ups. "One. Two. Three." And he was so tired and so sleepy and so full of food that when he started to push up for "Four," his arms became like rubber and there was no strength in them. He lay there on the floor, his eyes closed, sound asleep.

"Oh, no! What am I going to do?" the other brother moaned.

Just then, the chief sent his servant to get the dirty dishes. The servant walked in and saw the brother lying on the floor asleep.

He hurried away. Quickly the house was surrounded by the funeral drummers. There was the sound of a grave being dug and the people sang:

> *Dig a grave*
> *Dig it deep*
> *Someone in this village*
> *Fell asleep.*
>
> *That means he's dead,*
> *He's dead.*

That means he's dead,
Dead, dead.

The brother who was awake sang back to them:

Death has not come
Into this town
So please stop digging
That grave in the ground.

Wake up, my brother!
Wake up!
Wake up, my brother!
Please wake up!

He shook his brother very hard and his brother's eyes opened. "What's the matter? Let me alone."

"You'd better wake up. They think you're dead and are getting ready to bury you."

The other brother jumped up and rushed outside so that everyone could see that he was alive.

When the people saw him, they were terrified. "A dead man has come back to life!" they exclaimed.

The brothers explained that when people slept, they always came back to life. The people were amazed.

"You mean, sleep is not the same as death?"

"No, not at all," the brothers explained.

The people thought they would try this new thing called sleep. They went to bed and closed their eyes and were quickly asleep.

The next morning they were all very surprised and happy when they woke up and felt so wonderful.

They were grateful that the brothers had taught them how to sleep and the chief gave them a large sack of gold.

This time, the brothers did not argue because each had his own sack of gold and each realized, too, how much he needed the other.

The Woman
And The Tree
Children

NCE THERE WAS A WOMAN WHO HAD GROWN OLD and whose days had been filled with trouble. "Why have I had so many problems and troubles in my life?" she said to herself.

She thought and thought. "Perhaps it is because I did not have a husband and did not have children."

She decided to go to the medicine man and ask him to give her a husband and children.

The medicine man lived deep in the forest beneath a giant tree and it took the woman many hours to reach him.

"I have had a very unhappy life," she explained to the medicine man. "I think it is because I did not have a husband and children. So I have come to ask you to give me a husband and some children."

"I cannot give you both," he answered. "You must choose one or the other."

The woman thought for a long time. Finally she said, "Children."

"This is what you must do. Take some of your cooking pots into the forest until you find a fruit-bearing sycamore tree. Fill the pots with the fruit, leave the fruit-filled pots in your house and go for a walk."

"That is all?" the woman wanted to know.

"That is all," the medicine man said.

The woman did exactly as the medicine man had told her. She cleaned her pots until they shone like stars. Then she carried as many as her arms could hold into the woods until she came to a fruit-bearing sycamore tree. She climbed the tree and picked the fruit and filled her pots. The pots were very heavy but she carried them to her house and set them inside. Then she went for a walk until the sun began to set.

She returned to her house. As she came close, she heard voices, children's voices. She hurried along the path and there, the yard of her house was filled with happy children playing with one another.

When she walked into her house, she saw that the children had swept and cleaned the floor, washed and dried all the dishes, made the bed and brought the cattle in from the field. The woman was very happy.

Many months passed and the woman and the children lived peacefully together. Then, one day, something happened. It does not matter what. It was nothing important. Perhaps the woman had not slept well the night before, and was feeling tired and irritable that day. Perhaps something she had eaten was hurting her stomach.

In any event, one of the children did something — laughed too loudly for the woman's ears, dropped a dish or a glass and broke it, or something else. The woman yelled at the child.

"It is no wonder you did that. You are nothing but a child of the tree. You are all nothing but children of the tree! One can't expect any better from children born out of a tree."

The children became very quiet and still and did not say a word to the woman. Later that day the woman went to visit a friend. That evening when she came home, the children were not there. The house felt empty and lonely, and the woman cried and cried and cried.

The next day the woman went to the medicine man and asked him what she should do. He said he did not know.

"Should I go back to the fruit-bearing sycamore tree?" she wanted to know.

The medicine man shrugged and said he did not know what she could do.

The woman returned to her home and washed all the pots and carried them to the fruit-bearing sycamore tree. She climbed the tree and reached to pick the fruit.

But the skin of the fruit parted and revealed eyes, the eyes of the children. They stared at the woman and their eyes were filled with tears. They stared and stared until the woman climbed down from the tree and returned to her home.

And she lived in sadness for the rest of her life.

Why Monkeys Live In Trees

ONE DAY LEOPARD WAS LOOKING AT HIS REFLECTION in a pool of water. Looking at himself was Leopard's favorite thing in the world to do. Leopard gazed, wanting to be sure that every hair was straight and that all his spots were where they were supposed to be. This took many hours of looking at his reflection, which Leopard did not mind at all.

Finally he was satisfied that nothing was disturbing his handsomeness, and he turned away from the pool of water. At that exact moment, one of Leopard's children ran up to him.

"Daddy! Daddy! Are you going to be in the contest?"

"What contest?" Leopard wanted to know. If it was a beauty contest, of course he was going to be in it.

"I don't know. Crow the Messenger just flew by. She said that King Gorilla said there was going to be a contest."

Without another word, Leopard set off. He went north-by-northeast, made a right turn at the mulberry bush and traveled east-by-south-by-west until he came to a hole in the ground. He went around in a circle five times, and headed north-by-somersault until he came to a big clearing in the middle of the jungle and that's where King Gorilla was.

How Many Spots Does A Leopard Have?

King Gorilla sat at one end of the clearing on his throne. Opposite him, at the other side of the clearing, all the animals sat in a semicircle. In the middle, between King Gorilla and the animals, was a huge mound of what looked like black dust.

Leopard looked around with calm dignity. Then he strode regally over to his friend, Lion.

"What's that?" he asked, pointing to the mound of black dust.

"Don't know," Lion replied. "King Gorilla said he will give a pot of gold to whoever can eat it in one day. I can eat it in an hour."

Leopard laughed. "I'll eat it in a half hour."

It was Hippopotamus's turn to laugh. "As big as my mouth is, I'll eat that mound in one gulp."

The time came for the contest. King Gorilla had the animals pick numbers to see who would go in what order. To everybody's dismay, Hippopotamus drew Number 1.

Hippopotamus walked over to the mound of black dust. It was bigger than he had thought. It was much too big to eat in one gulp. Nonetheless, Hippopotamus opened his mouth as wide as he could, and that was very wide indeed, and took a mouthful of the black dust.

He started chewing. Suddenly he leaped straight into the air and screamed. He screamed so loudly that it knocked the ears off the chickens and that's why to this day chickens don't have ears.

Hippopotamus screamed and Hippopotamus yelled. Hippopotamus roared and Hippopotamus bellowed. Then he started sneezing and crying and tears rolled down his face like he was standing in the shower. Hippopotamus ran to the river and drank as much water as he could, and that was very much, indeed, to cool his mouth and tongue and throat.

The animals didn't understand what had happened to Hippopotamus, but they didn't care. They were happy because they still had a chance to win the pot of gold. Of course, if they had known that the mound of black dust was really a mound of black pepper, maybe they wouldn't have wanted the gold.

Nobody was more happy than Leopard because he had drawn Number 2. He walked up to the black mound and sniffed at it.

"AAAAAAAAACHOOOOOOO!" Leopard didn't like that but then he remembered the pot of gold. He opened his mouth wide, took a mouthful and started chewing and swallowing.

Leopard leaped straight into the air, did a back double flip and screamed. He yelled and he roared and he bellowed and, finally, he started sneezing and crying, tears rolling down his face like a waterfall. Leopard ran to the river and washed out his mouth and throat and tongue.

Lion was next, and the same thing happened to him as it did to all the animals. Finally only Monkey remained.

Monkey approached King Gorilla. "I know I can eat all of whatever that is, but after each mouthful, I'll need to lie down in the tall grasses and rest."

King Gorilla said that was okay.

Monkey went to the mound, took a tiny bit of pepper on his tongue, swallowed, and went into the tall grasses. A few minutes later, Monkey came out, took a little more, swallowed it, and went into the tall grasses.

Soon the pile was almost gone. The animals were astonished to see Monkey doing what they had not been able to do.

How Many Spots Does A Leopard Have?

Leopard couldn't believe it either. He climbed a tree and stretched out on a sturdy limb to get a better view. From his limb high in the tree Leopard could see into the tall grasses where Monkey went to rest. Wait a minute! Leopard thought something was suddenly wrong with his eyes because he thought he saw a hundred monkeys hiding in the tall grasses.

He rubbed his eyes and looked another look. There wasn't anything wrong with his eyes. There *were* a hundred monkeys in the tall grasses and they all looked alike!

Just then, there was the sound of loud applause. King Gorilla announced that Monkey had won the contest and the pot of gold.

Leopard growled a growl so scary that even King Gorilla was frightened. Leopard wasn't thinking about anybody except the monkeys. He took a long and beautiful leap from the tree right smack into the middle of the tall grasses where the monkeys were hiding.

The monkeys ran in all directions. When the other animals saw monkeys running from the grasses, they realized that the monkeys had tricked them and starting chasing them. Even King Gorilla joined in the chase. He wanted his gold back.

The only way the monkeys could escape was to climb to the very tops of the tallest trees where no one else, not even Leopard, could climb.

And that's why monkeys live in trees to this very day.

What Is The Most Important Part Of The Body?

WHEN GOD CREATED PEOPLE, HE MADE ALL THE PARTS of the body with great care — Head, Eyes, Ears, Nose, Mouth, Throat, Feet, Hands, Heart, Stomach, Tongue and all the rest.

Then God told the other parts what their jobs were.

Feet's job was to stand firmly on the ground.

Hands' job was to hold and to touch.

Nose's job was to smell.

Eyes' job was to see.

Mouth's job was to chew and Throat would swallow.

Heart's job was to pump blood to every part of the body.

Head's job was to think.

Tongue's job was to taste and speak.

And Stomach's job was to take care of all the food that entered the body and to be the king.

All the parts of the body did their jobs perfectly and for a while they were content. However, after a while they began to complain.

Throat was the first. "Hands, all the food you put in me doesn't stay for one second. Stomach grabs it and takes it for himself. I think we need a new king, someone who'll be fair."

Teeth agreed. "We chew the food, but Stomach takes it.

45

What Is The Most Important Part Of The Body?

We want a king who will not be so selfish."

"At least you get to touch the food," said Eyes. "All we can ever do is look at it."

Feet snorted. "At least you get to see the food. All I do is walk to it. I never see it. I never touch it. And I certainly don't know what it tastes like."

All the parts of the body agreed that they needed a new king, someone who would treat everyone fairly. They decided to talk to God.

"We want a new king. King Stomach is greedy. He only cares about himself. He never thinks of us."

God was disturbed to hear this. He thought for a while. Finally he reached a decision. "What you should do is this: Hold a meeting and decide whom you want for your new king. However, before and after your meeting, don't eat anything. Don't eat anything until I come in two days. Then you can tell me who your new king will be."

The parts of the body thought this was a good idea. "We'll show King Stomach that he can't do without us. We won't give him any food. Then he'll see that being king is no fun!"

They started discussing who should be the new king. Soon, the discussing turned to debating and, after a while, the debating became arguing. Then it became all three and they discussed and debated and argued from morning until the night had started gobbling up the day.

The morning of the second day came. God was going to come soon and they had not decided on a new king. But they couldn't decide anything. They were too hungry!

"Left Eye. You be the king," said Mouth weakly.

Left Eye said, "I can't see well this morning. A king cannot have weak eyes. Left Foot, what about you?"

47

Left Foot said, "I am so hungry, I cannot stand very steadily. How can I be king?"

All the parts of the body were feeling weak and none of them wanted to be king.

Mouth said, "Perhaps we should let Stomach remain king." Everyone agreed.

God came. "Have you decided who is going to be the new king?"

They told him that they did not want a new king. "We see now that Stomach divides the food equally and each part of the body gets what it needs to do its job."

God told Hands to cook a broth for Stomach. This was done. Hands fed the broth to Mouth and Teeth, and the broth flowed over them and continued down Throat until it reached Stomach. Stomach distributed the broth to the other parts of the body.

In a little while, things were no longer blurry to Eyes. Feet started wiggling its toes. Mouth began humming a tune. All the parts of the body felt like themselves again and were very happy.

One part of the body was not happy, though. It didn't mind that Stomach was king. It just wanted the other parts to recognize that it was important, too.

It decided that it would wait. One day it would have the opportunity to prove how important it was.

That day came when the beautiful Princess Maki became seriously ill. She was the only child of the King and Queen, the only heir to the throne of the kingdom.

She lay in bed with a mysterious illness and if something was not done, she would die.

The royal physicians examined her from head to foot, from

foot to head, from hair to toenail. They consulted their medical books. They consulted among themselves.

When they finished studying their medical books, when they were done talking among themselves, they agreed that there was only one cure that would save the life of the beloved princess.

"Your Majesties," they reported to the King and Queen, "there is only one thing in the whole round world that will heal the princess. Unfortunately it is a thing impossible to get."

"What is that?" the Queen demanded to know.

"The milk of a lioness."

"What?" roared the King. "That is impossible!"

"Precisely, Your Majesty," said the physicians.

"But the princess is our only child," said the Queen. "If she dies there will be no one to rule the people after we are gone. Our country will be taken over by our enemies."

What were they going to do?

The King issued a decree. "I will give one half of my kingdom to the man who gets the milk of a lioness for the Princess Maki."

News of the decree spread through the kingdom. All agreed it would be wonderful to have one half of the kingdom, but no one could get the milk of a lioness. They were very sad because it meant that the beautiful young princess would die.

However, high in the mountains lived a young man named Kwame. When he heard the decree, his heart became strong with determination. He would save the life of the beautiful princess.

He left his mountain village and descended to the plain where the lions and lionesses lived. He found a lioness who had recently given birth and was nursing her young.

How was he going to get some of her milk? If he approached her, she would think he was threatening her young and she would attack and kill him.

Kwame had an idea! He killed a goat and threw a piece of the meat to the lioness. She ate it. The next day Kwame did the same, moving a little closer to the lioness. Each day he came closer and closer to the lioness, until she was taking the goat meat from his hand.

He spoke softly and gently to the lioness, stroking her until she purred with contentment. Then he milked her.

Kwame started for the palace carrying the milk of the lioness in a large jug.

The parts of the body were very proud of themselves because each had played an important role in getting the milk.

"I could see how to find the lioness," said Eyes.

"Yes, but hearing her purr, I knew when it was safe to milk her," said Ears.

"Who took you to the lioness, and who would have taken you away from there if she had attacked?" Feet proclaimed.

"But who actually got the milk from the lioness and who is now carrying it to save the life of the princess?" Hands declared proudly.

Each part of the body talked about how important it was. Each part, that is, except Tongue. "Wait. Just wait," Tongue said to itself. "I'll show you who's important."

When Kwame reached the palace, he went immediately to the King and Queen. Now it was Tongue's turn.

"Your Majesties, I have brought you the very thing and the only thing that will save the life of the beautiful princess — the milk of a dog!"

What Is The Most Important Part Of The Body?

"What?!" yelled the King. "You dare come here and make fun of us! Guards! Arrest this man and hang him at once!"

Tongue turned to the other parts of the body. "See. With one word I have the power to determine if you live or die. Admit that I am very important and I'll save us from being killed."

The other parts of the body agreed immediately that Tongue was very, very important!

Then Tongue spoke again. "Your Majesties, please forgive me. In my eagerness to be of service and to save the life of the young and beautiful princess, I tripped over my words. This milk is indeed that of a lioness. Have your physicians give it to the princess. If it does not heal her, my life is in your hands."

The King and the Queen had the physicians give the milk to the princess. Within moments, Princess Maki walked into the throne room in all of her beauty, cured of her mysterious illness.

Princess Maki and Kwame looked at each other and fell in love. Soon thereafter they were married.

Tongue took his place as the most important part of the body because everyone agreed that he had the greatest power for good and evil.

When Maki and Kwame came to be Queen and King, they used their tongues for good.

May we do the same.

How Many Spots Does A Leopard Have?

NE MORNING LEOPARD WAS DOING WHAT HE enjoyed doing most. He was looking at his reflection in the lake. How handsome he was! How magnificent was his coat! And, ah! The spots on his coat! Was there anything in creation more superb?

Leopard's rapture was broken when the water in the lake began moving. Suddenly Crocodile's ugly head appeared above the surface.

Leopard jumped back. Not that he was afraid. Crocodile would not bother him. But then again, one could never be too sure about Crocodile.

"Good morning, Leopard," Crocodile said. "Looking at yourself again, I see. You are the most vain creature in all of creation."

Leopard was not embarrassed. "If you were as handsome as I am, if you had such beautiful spots, you, too, would be vain."

"Spots! Who needs spots? You're probably so in love with your spots that you spend all your time counting them."

Now there was an idea that had not occurred to Leopard. "What a wonderful idea!" he exclaimed. "I would very much like to know how many spots I have." He stopped. "But there are far too many for me to count myself."

The truth was that Leopard didn't know how to count. "Perhaps you will count them for me, Crocodile?"

"Not on your life!" answered Crocodile. "I have better things to do than count spots." He slapped his tail angrily and dove beneath the water.

Leopard chuckled. "Crocodile doesn't know how to count, either."

Leopard walked along the lakeshore until he met Weasel. "Good morning, Weasel. Would you count my spots for me?"

"Who? Me? Count? Sure. One-two-three-four."

"Great!" exclaimed Leopard. "You can count."

Weasel shook his head. "But I can't. What made you think that I could?"

"But you just did. You said, 'One-two-three-four.' That's counting."

Weasel shook his head again. "Counting is much more difficult than that. There is something that comes after four, but I don't know what it is."

"Oh," said Leopard. "I wonder who knows what comes after four."

"Well, if you ask at the lake when all the animals come to drink, you will find someone who can count."

"You are right, Weasel! And I will give a grand prize to the one who tells me how many spots I have."

"What a great idea!" Weasel agreed.

That afternoon all the animals were gathered at the lake to drink. Leopard announced that he would give a magnificent prize to the one who could count his spots.

Elephant said he should be first since he was the biggest and the oldest.

How Many Spots Does A Leopard Have?

"One-two-three-four-five-six-seven-eight-nine-ten," Elephant said very loudly and with great speed. He took a deep breath and began again. "One-two-three-four-five-si — "

"No! No! No!" the other animals interrupted. "You've already counted to ten once."

Elephant looked down his long trunk at the other animals. "I beg your pardon. I would appreciate it if you would not interrupt me when I am counting. You made me forget where I was. Now, where was I? I know I was somewhere in the second ten."

"The second ten?" asked Antelope. "What's that?"

"The numbers that come after the first ten, of course. I don't much care for those 'teen' things, thirteen, fourteen, and what have you. It is eminently more sensible to count ten twice and that makes twenty. That is multiplication."

None of the other animals knew what Elephant was talking about.

"Why don't you start over again?" suggested Cow.

Elephant began again and he counted ten twice and stopped. He frowned and looked very confused. Finally he said, "Leopard has more than twenty spots."

"How many more than twenty?" Leopard wanted to know.

Elephant frowned more. "A lot." Then he brightened. "In fact, you have so many more spots than twenty that I simply don't have time to count them now. I have an important engagement I mustn't be late for." Elephant started to walk away.

"Ha! Ha! Ha!" laughed Mule. "I bet Elephant doesn't know how to count higher than twenty."

Mule was right.

"Can *you* count above twenty?" Leopard asked Mule.

How Many Spots Does A Leopard Have?

"Who? Me? I can only count to four because that's how many legs I have."

Leopard sighed. "Can *anyone* count above twenty?" he asked plaintively.

Bear said, "Well, once I counted up to fifty. Is that high enough?"

Leopard shrugged. "I don't know. It might be. Why don't you try and we will see."

Bear agreed. "I'll start at your tail. One-two-three-four-five-six. . . . Hm. Is that one spot or two spots?"

All the animals crowded around to get a close look. They argued for some time and finally agreed that it should only count as one.

"So, where was I?" asked Bear.

"Five," answered Turkey.

"It was six, you turkey," said Chicken.

"Better start again," suggested Crow.

Bear started again and got as far as eleven. "Eleven. That's a beautiful spot right there, Leopard."

"Which one?" Leopard wanted to know.

"Right there. Oh, dear. Or was it that spot there? They're both exquisite. My, my. I don't know where I left off counting. I must start again."

Bear counted as far as twenty-nine this time and then stopped suddenly. "Now, what comes after twenty-nine?"

"I believe thirty does," offered Turtle.

"That's right!" exclaimed Bear. "Now, where did I leave off?"

"You were still on the tail," offered Lion.

"Yes, but was that the twenty-ninth spot, or was it this one here?"

How Many Spots Does A Leopard Have?

The animals started arguing again.

"You'd better start again," suggested Cow.

"Start what again?" asked Rabbit who had just arrived.

The animals explained to Rabbit about the difficulty they were having in counting Leopard's spots.

"Is that all?" Rabbit said. "I know the answer to that."

"You do?" all the animals, including Leopard, exclaimed at once.

"Certainly. It's really quite simple." Rabbit pointed to one of Leopard's spots. "This one is dark." He pointed to another. "This one is light. Dark, light, dark, light, dark, light." Rabbit continued in this way until he had touched all of Leopard's spots.

"It's simple," he concluded. "Leopard has only two spots — dark ones and light ones."

All the animals remarked on how smart Rabbit was, all of them, that is, except Leopard. He knew something was wrong with how Rabbit counted, but unless he learned to count for himself, he would never know what it was.

Leopard had no choice but to give Rabbit the magnificent prize.

What was it?

What else except a picture of Leopard himself!

57

The Wonderful Healing Leaves

NCE UPON A TIME THERE WAS A KING AND QUEEN who had three beautiful daughters. The king and queen wanted their daughters to marry rich and handsome princes.

When it was time for the first daughter to marry, she married a very handsome and very wealthy prince.

When it came time for the second daughter to marry, she married a very, very handsome and very, very wealthy prince.

When it was time for the third daughter to marry, she fell in love with a very ugly and very poor man. The king and queen were upset and forbade their daughter to marry him.

The princess loved the ugly and poor man deeply, because his heart was rich with kindness and his soul was beautiful in its purity. So the princess sneaked away from the palace and married the man she loved.

When she returned and told her parents what she had done, they were furious. "How dare you disobey us!" the king roared. "You and your husband are ordered to leave this palace and never set foot here again!"

So the princess and her husband moved into a tiny house in the town and, though they were poor, they were very happy in their love for each other.

How Many Spots Does A Leopard Have?

One morning not too many months later the king awoke and discovered that while he was sleeping, he had gone blind. His eyes were open, but he could not see.

The king called all the doctors in the kingdom to examine him. They did, but none of them knew how to restore his sight.

Finally a doctor came from the farthest city in the kingdom. He examined the king carefully. "Your Majesty, there is only one cure for your blindness."

"Well, what is it?"

"In the Land of No Return there is a tree whose leaves can heal blindness."

"I will send someone at once to get me some of those healing leaves."

"You should know, Sire, that no one who has gone to the Land of No Return to get these leaves has ever returned. That is why it is called the Land of No Return."

The king understood, but what other choice did he have? He called the two princes who had married his daughters and told them that he wanted them to go to the Land of No Return and bring him the wonderful healing leaves that would restore his sight.

"You should know," the king continued, "that no one has returned from this land. If you do return with the leaves, I will give each of you one third of my kingdom. However, if you come back and do not have the leaves, I will have you hanged."

The two princes took speedy and strong horses from the royal stable and set forth immediately.

The youngest daughter heard about her father's blindness and the wonderful healing leaves. She went to the palace secretly and met her mother who missed her deeply.

"Mother, I know that you and father have rejected me because of my husband, but he is a good man with a pure heart and soul. If anyone can return with the leaves that will restore father's sight, it is he. Please give him a chance."

"You understand the conditions?"

"Yes, Mother, and he accepts those conditions."

"Very well," the queen said. She saw to it that the husband of the third daughter was given a lame and weak horse and he left for the Land of No Return.

The two princes had arrived in the province next to the Land of No Return. They learned that many had tried to reach the tree on which the wonderful healing leaves grew, but the road to the tree was guarded by a dragon and a viper and they destroyed anyone who came near.

The two princes became very frightened and did not know what to do. It was impossible to get the leaves. However, if they returned to the king without the leaves, he would hang them. What were they going to do?

They would stay at the inn until they decided. Perhaps they would stay at the inn for the rest of their lives. That would be safer than letting the king hang them. So they made themselves very comfortable at the inn, eating rich food and drinking fine wine.

Two weeks later, the man who had married the third princess arrived at the inn on his lame and weak horse. When he entered the inn, he recognized the two princes sitting before the fireplace drinking wine. The two princes did not recognize him, however, and he did not tell them who he was.

The next morning he went through the province asking people about the Land of No Return and the tree with the wonderful healing leaves.

How Many Spots Does A Leopard Have?

People told him that the road to the tree was guarded by a dragon and a viper who destroyed anyone who came near.

The ugly and poor man was not afraid. Because he did not show any fear and seemed determined to do what no one had ever done, people told him, "Well, there *is* one person who knows how to reach the tree of the wonderful healing leaves without being destroyed by the dragon and the viper."

"Who is that?"

"The giant who lives in the valley below. However, the giant is a terrible man. In fact, he eats everyone who comes within reach."

The ugly and poor man was not afraid. He got on his horse and set out for the valley below where the giant lived. He rode until he reached a house as high as the highest mountain. The door of the house was so high that the ugly and poor man could not see the doorknob. How big was the giant if the door to his house was that large?

The ugly and poor man was not afraid. He knocked loudly on the door. The wife of the giant opened it. The man looked like a dot from her great height.

"You must leave immediately," she shouted down to him. "If my husband finds you when he comes back, he will eat you."

"I must speak with him," the man shouted up. "I need directions to the Land of No Return and the tree with the wonderful healing leaves."

The woman saw that he was determined to speak with the giant, so she let him in and hid him under the bed.

Before long the giant returned. He sniffed the air. "I smell the meat and blood of a man. Where is he?" the giant roared.

"Your nose must be playing tricks on you, dear," the giant's wife said.

"I know man-meat when I smell it," he said.

The ugly and poor man came out from under the bed. "Indeed you do and I congratulate you. What a very fine nose you have to smell something as tiny and puny as me."

"Thank you very much," the giant said, surprised at being addressed so courteously.

"You are my host, giant. I am your guest, which means that you may do with me what you wish. However, before you eat me, if that is your desire, let me tell you a story."

The giant was amazed that something so ugly and so poor and so small could be so brave. "All right. It's been a long time since anybody told me a story."

So the ugly and poor man told the giant about the king's blindness. "And that is why I need to go to the Land of No Return and find the tree of the wonderful healing leaves."

The giant was impressed. "Because you were not afraid of me and are not afraid to go to the Land of No Return, I will not eat you. You are the first man I've ever met who was not a coward." The giant invited him to stay for dinner and to be his guest overnight.

The next morning the ugly and poor man and the giant arose early.

"This is what you must do," the giant told him. "Ride for seven days. You will come to a crossroads. On one side there is a sign that reads, 'A happy journey.' On the other side there is a sign that reads, 'He who follows this path shall not return.' That is the road you take. Stay on that road until it comes to a dead end.

"This is the first point of danger. When you reach the dead end, you must say, 'What a beautiful path! Had I all the horses of the king I would come and dance here!' The dead end will disappear and the road will continue.

How Many Spots Does A Leopard Have?

"Next you will come to a valley filled with huge and poisonous snakes. No man has ever passed through it. When you come to the valley of the poisonous snakes, you should say, 'What a beautiful valley filled with honey! If only someone brought some of this honey to the palace of the king, he would gladly eat it!' The snakes will disappear, and you can continue on.

"Next you will come to a valley filled with blood and many beasts. No man has ever passed through it. When you come to the valley of blood and many beasts, you must say, 'What tasty butter! Had I the bread of the king, I would spread this tasty butter on it!' The valley will dry up and you can continue on your way.

"Next you will come to a palace. The palace is guarded by a dragon and a viper. Look at them closely. If their eyes are open, they are asleep. If their eyes are closed, they are wide awake. Wait until they are asleep, that is, wait until their eyes are open. Then walk past them and into the palace. Walk down the corridor and you will come to the queen's door. You will recognize the queen's door because there are four lions that guard it. Look at them closely. If their eyes are open, they are asleep; if their eyes are closed, they are awake. The door to the queen's chamber is made out of bells. When the door is opened, the bells ring and the lions awake. Here are two packages of cotton. When the eyes of the lions are open, put the cotton around the clappers of the bells and enter the queen's chamber. Inside, the queen will be asleep. When she sleeps, the lions sleep.

"Beside the queen's bed grows the tree with the wonderful healing leaves. Fill one bag with leaves and stuff as many as you can in your pockets. The wonderful healing leaves are precious. Then go over to the queen and take the ring off her finger and put your ring on her finger and her ring on your finger. Then go. On your way back, do everything you did before, but this time it will be in reverse order."

The poor and ugly man listened closely to the giant's instructions. "Thank you, friend giant. I will do as you have told me."

"Good luck," the giant wished him.

He set off and followed the giant's instructions. He continued on the path that ended and crossed the valley of poisonous snakes. He crossed the valley of blood and many beasts and eventually reached the palace. There he waited until the eyes of the dragon and the viper were open and hurried inside the palace. Outside the door to the queen's chamber he waited until the eyes of the lions opened, and he muffled the bells on the door and hurried inside. Beside the queen's bed he saw the tree with the wonderful healing leaves. Its branches reached to the top of the sky-high ceiling and its roots grew through the floor and beneath.

He filled a bag with the leaves and filled his pockets, too. Then he exchanged rings with the queen and returned from the Land of No Return, doing everything in reverse. Finally he came to the inn where the two princes were staying.

When the princes saw the ugly and poor man carrying a sack filled with leaves, they became suspicious. "What do you have there, my good fellow?" they asked.

The poor and ugly man told them the entire story. However, he forgot to mention that he had stuffed his pockets with the wonderful healing leaves or that he had exchanged rings with the queen.

That night while the ugly and poor man slept, the two princes bought a potion from an evil witch. They sneaked into the room of the ugly and poor man, rubbed the potion in his eyes and he was blinded. Then, they put him in a sack and left him in a closet.

They took the bag of healing leaves and hurried back to the palace of the king. The king rubbed some of the wonderful healing leaves on his eyes and his sight was restored! The king was grateful. He kept his promise and gave one third of his kingdom to each of the two princes.

Meanwhile, at the inn, the ugly and poor man awoke and found himself blind and tied in a sack. He was not afraid, however, and after much work he freed himself from the sack. Once he was free, he remembered that he had filled his pockets with wonderful healing leaves. He rubbed a few on his eyes and he could see again.

He returned to his wife, the king's youngest daughter. "I have returned with the wonderful healing leaves," he told her.

She laughed at him. "The two princes who married my older sisters brought the leaves back before you. My father, the king, can now see and he has given a third of his kingdom to each of my sister's husbands. There is nothing for us because you were so slow."

He understood everything that had happened but said nothing.

When the queen of the Land of No Return finally awoke, she saw that her ring had been taken and another put there in its stead. She looked at the tree and saw that it had been stripped of all its leaves.

The queen arose from her bed, clapped her hands four times and her flying carpet came to her. She got on it and flew over the world, going high and low, looking for the one who had taken her ring and the leaves. Eventually she heard of a king who had been miraculously cured of his blindness.

She went immediately to the king's palace and stood before the king. "I am queen of the Land of No Return. If you do not tell me how you cured your blindness, I will have a dragon destroy your kingdom."

The king was afraid of the queen of the Land of No Return, and he told the two princes to tell her how his blindness was cured. The princes hurried forward with the bag and the leaves that remained.

"Where did you get these leaves?"

"We found them on a tree in the forest," the princes stammered.

"You are lying!" the queen yelled. "I will call my dragon to destroy the kingdom."

"All right, all right," said the princes. "We took them from a very ugly and very poor man."

"Who is this man?"

"We do not know," the princes said.

"You are lying!"

"No, no. We are telling the truth!"

"I know who the man is," said the queen, the mother of the three princesses. "It is the man who married our youngest daughter."

"Send for him!" the queen of the Land of No Return ordered. It was done.

The poor and ugly man and his wife, the youngest daughter, arrived at the palace.

"What do you know about these leaves?" the queen of the Land of No Return wanted to know.

He told her the story. He showed her the leaves he had in the pocket of his jacket. Then he held out his hand and the queen of the Land of No Return saw her ring on his finger and she knew he was telling the truth.

"And how did these two princes get the leaves from you?"

He told the rest of the story. Then he gave the queen back her ring, but she did not return his. "I will keep your ring so that I can remember the bravest man I have ever met. And as a reward for your bravery, I will permit you to keep the leaves."

She mounted her flying carpet and flew back to the Land of No Return.

The king understood now that the two princes had stolen the leaves and tried to harm the husband of his youngest daughter. He took back the parts of the kingdom he had given them and took away all the rest of their wealth and banished them and their wives, his two older daughters, from the palace. The two princes and their wives lived in poverty and were very unhappy.

He asked the youngest daughter and her husband to forgive him. The king gave the ugly and poor but very brave young man many riches and made him a prince. When the king and queen died, the poor and ugly man, who was now a wealthy and handsome prince, became king and his wife became queen. They ruled the kingdom with wisdom and lived happily ever after.

Author's
Note

THE FOLKTALES I HAVE TOLD IN THIS BOOK ARE FROM THE AFRICAN AND Jewish traditions. Although I am of African and Jewish ancestry, I am also an American. The culture in which I live is very different from the societies and cultures that created these tales.

But that is what is so wonderful about stories. We can understand and enjoy them regardless of their place of origin. That is so because there is a level of human experience called universal, meaning there are experiences that are common to us all, and it does not matter how far apart from each other we may live on the globe.

In rewriting these tales, I have chosen to remove references to things that did not communicate to me as an American, references that were foreign and served to obstruct my enjoyment of the story. By so doing I have chosen to emphasize the universal dimension of the story over the cultural where it was not possible to keep the two fused into one whole.

To put it another way, I have done what any storyteller does: I have fitted the story to my mouth and tongue. Thus, the language and images of the stories are mine. I hope that you will fit these stories to your mouth and tongue.

The following notes describe how my versions differ from the originals.

"Why The Sun And Moon Live In The Sky" is from the Efik-Ibibio people of Africa and I found the tale in Susan Feldman's *African Myths and Tales* and *African Folktales* by Paul Radin. In the original story the Sun builds a "compound" for the water to stay in when it comes to visit. I changed this to "large house." I also modified the reasons why the Sun and the Moon live in the sky, as the original story does not address the question of why the Sun and Moon did not come out of the sky when the water went away.

"The Bird That Made Milk" is a Xosa tale found in Radin's *African Folktales*. In the original story, there were two cultural elements with which I was not wholly comfortable. One was that the man's wife does not have a name and is referred to solely as his wife. The second was the appearance in the story of a cannibal. I gave Masilo's wife a name, Adisa, and I substituted the Monster Who Eats Children for the cannibal. The major change is in the ending. In the original, one large bird rescues the children and returns them to the village. I have substituted a flock of birds that give milk who, in effect, save the entire village. In the original story, the element of the famine is forgotten and is left unresolved.

"The Monster Who Swallowed Everything" is from Susan Feldman's *African Myths and Tales* where it is called "The Swallowing Monster." It is from the Basuto people. In the original, when Dit-a-Lane begins to cut into the monster, he accidentally cuts the leg of a man who had been swallowed by the monster. That man bears a grudge against Dit-a-Lane, and the story continues to tell of the attempts this man makes to kill Dit-a-Lane, and eventually he succeeds. Clearly this ending reflects something within Basuto culture that is beyond me. I liked the story up to its happy ending and that is what I am comfortable telling.

"Tug-Of-War" is a story from the Fan people and I found it in Feldman's *African Myths and Tales* where it is called "A Tug of War." I made no essential changes except to intensify the confidence of Turtle.

"Why Dogs Chase Cats" is a Jewish legend. A version can be found in Louis Ginzberg's *Legends of the Jews*. I made no essential changes except to supply more character motivation and personality.

"The Town Where Snoring Was Not Allowed" is from the Mende people and I found it in the Feldman collection. The original story is about two strangers. I changed them to two brothers because I did not know why two strangers would be traveling together. I also changed the song and created the argument at the end of the story.

"The Town Where Sleeping Was Not Allowed" is a Hausa tale from the Feldman collection. I have made it a companion tale to the one preceding because of the similarities. In the Hausa tale the protagonists are a woman who goes to visit her daughter who lives in the town where no one is allowed to sleep. The story also has references to a "corpse mat," which I omitted since I didn't know what it was. In the Feldman collection, the story continues with the mother visiting her other daughter who lives in a town where no one is allowed to urinate. In the Radin collection there is a version of this story, except that the second part has the mother visiting her other daughter in a town where no one is allowed to spit. I have omitted the second part of the story.

"The Woman And The Tree Children" is a Masai tale from the Radin collection, where it is called "The Woman and the Children of the Sycamore Tree." I have made no essential changes.

"Why Monkeys Live In Trees" is a Ngoni story found in Geraldine Elliot's *The Long Grass Whispers*, where it is called "The Barrel of Water." I have made no essential changes.

"What Is The Most Important Part Of The Body?" combines two stories, one African and one Jewish. The first part of the story is from the Yarwin-Mehnsonoh people and I found it in Peter Dorliae's collection *Animals Mourn for Da Leopard*, where it is called "King Stomach Wins the Contest." The second part of the story is a Jewish legend from Peninnah Schram's *Jewish Stories One Generation Tells Another*, where it is called "The Great Debate." In that version it is the King of Persia who falls ill. I have created the characters of the Princess Maki and Kwame.

"How Many Spots Does A Leopard Have?" is adapted from Geraldine Elliot's *The Long Grass Whispers*. I made no essential changes.

"The Wonderful Healing Leaves" is adapted from Howard Schwartz's *Elijah's Violin and Other Jewish Fairy Tales*. In that version the hero is merely poor and is called "the lad."

Bibliography

Dorliae, Peter G. *Animals Mourn for Da Leopard and Other West African Tales.* New York: Bobbs-Merrill, 1970.

Elliot, Geraldine. *The Long Grass Whispers: A Book of African Folk Tales.* New York: Shocken, 1968.

Feldman, Susan. *African Myths and Tales.* New York: Dell, 1963.

Ginzberg, Louis. *Legends of the Jews.* Seven volumes. Philadelphia: Jewish Publication Society, 1946.

Radin, Paul. *African Folktales.* Princeton/Bollingen, 1970.

Schram, Peninnah. *Jewish Stories One Generation Tells Another.* Northvale, New Jersey: Jason Aronson, Inc., 1987.

Schwartz, Howard. *Elijah Violin and Other Jewish Fairy Tales.* New York: Harper & Row, 1985.